Alex T. Smith

ASTRID AND THE SPACE CADETS!

Attack of the Snailiens!

MACMILLAN CHILDREN'S BOOKS

Published 2024 by Macmillan Children's Books
an imprint of Pan Macmillan
The Smithson, 6–9 Briset Street, London, EC1M 5NR
EU representative: Macmillan Publishers Ireland Limited, 1st Floor,
The Liffey Trust Centre, 117–126 Sheriff Street Upper, Dublin 1 D01 YC43
Associated companies throughout the world
www.panmacmillan.com

ISBN 978-1-0350-1974-8
Text copyright and illustrations © Alex T. Smith 2024

1 3 5 7 9 8 6 4 2

A CIP catalogue record for this book is available from the British Library.

Printed and bound by CPI Group (UK) Ltd, Croydon CR0 4YY

This book is for
Space Cadet Connor.
With love from Uncle Alex.

MEET THE **SPACE ✳ CADETS!**

✳ **ASTRID:** A small human person! (*She/Her.*)

✳ **BERYL:** A pink alien from the planet SPANGLE. (*She/Her.*)

SPACE ✳ CADETS!

THEY ARE AN ELITE(ish) GROUP OF

INTERGALACTIC HELPERS

AND FINDER-OUTERS, WHO
ZOOM ACROSS THE UNIVERSE TO
SOLVE ANY PROBLEM,

BIG

OR SMALL!

ARE YOU READY TO BLAST OFF
AND JOIN THEM?

YES?

WELL, HURRY UP INTO THE
SPACESHIP THEN – WE'VE GOT
A MISSION TO COMPLETE!

A long time ago

(but also right now)

in a galaxy far, far away

(that is also actually *this* galaxy)

on the planet of Earth,

there lives a girl called . . .

1969
ROCKET
DRIVE

ASTRID ATOMIC!

And every night Astrid
gets ready for bed.

She has a bath.
She puts on her pyjamas.
She reads a book.

She says goodnight to her dads.
She turns out her light.

But she *doesn't* go to sleep . . .

She waits.

She waits until
the clock strikes
midnight and
then . . .

Up she jumps, out of bed!
Off come her pyjamas,
(revealing her Space Cadet
uniform underneath!),

She climbs into her wardrobe
(which is really an Intergalactic
Transporter Pod),

And . . .

5...

4...

3...

2...

1...

She blasts off to meet
the Space Cadets,
just in time to be briefed
by The Chief.

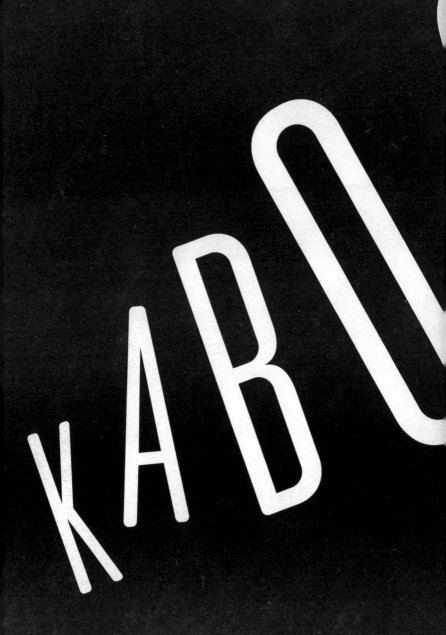

A MESSAGE FROM THE SPACE CADETS' BOSS, THE CHIEF:

CRACKLE . . . CRACKLE . . .

'Greetings, Space Cadets!

'And welcome to another starlit day here in the universe.

'I have an important mission for you today. The edges of the Milky Way are looking very untidy.

There's quite a bit of rubbish out there.

'Your mission is to give the place a good tidy-up. Make it spick and span and neat and clean.

'And remember, if you complete your task, you'll get another gold star for your cosmic star chart. The more stars on your star chart, the closer you are to getting the Great Galaxy Prize!

'Good luck, Space Cadets! I know you can do it.'

CRACKLE . . . CRACKLE . . .

'EASY-PEASY!' said Astrid, after The Chief had disappeared from the screen with a fizzle. 'The edge of the Milky Way can't be THAT messy, can it? We'll have it shipshape in a jiffy!'

'**ZOINK!**' said Zoink, in a very giddy fashion.

'That's right, Zoink!' agreed Astrid. 'We'll have a bright new shiny star for our star chart too!'

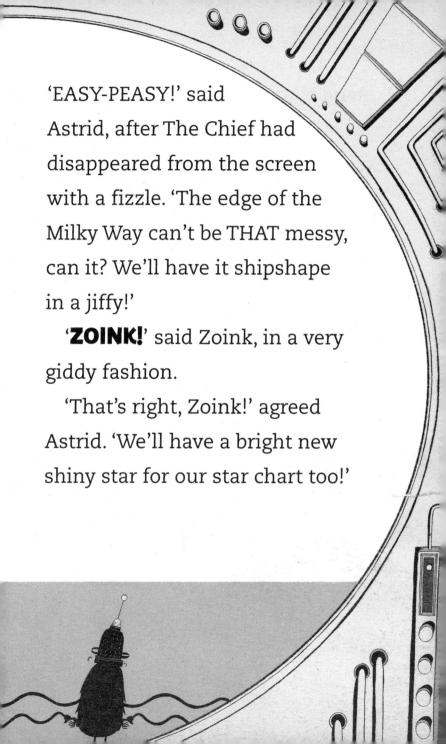

Beryl clapped her hands to her cheeks. She turned a shade of pink exactly fifteen times brighter than her usual bright pinkness.

'**Ooooh I love gold stars!**' she cried.
'**They're so bright and twinkly!**'

'And we're getting closer to
getting the Great Galaxy Prize!' said
Astrid, looking at the star chart.
Her eyes sparkled with excitement
behind her glasses.

'I wonder what the prize is.'
said Professor Quackers.
'I hope it's doughnuts!'

All of the Space Cadets
licked their lips and said,
'MMMMMMMMMMMMMMM' as
they thought about doughnuts.

Then it was time to get to work.

'Well, we'd better set off!' said Astrid, eagerly. She loved missions. 'Is everyone ready?'

'READY!' shouted Beryl in her Outdoor Voice.

'**ZOINK!**' cried Zoink.

'Ready,' honked Professor Quackers.

'Then let's go,' said
Astrid.

And the Space Cadets all
leapt into their seats and CLICK-
CLICKED their seat belts.

Zoink was the driver, so they took
the controls and cried, '**ZOINK!**'
(which meant 'YEEE-HAAAAAAH!').

Then they pressed a big red
button on the dashboard labelled:

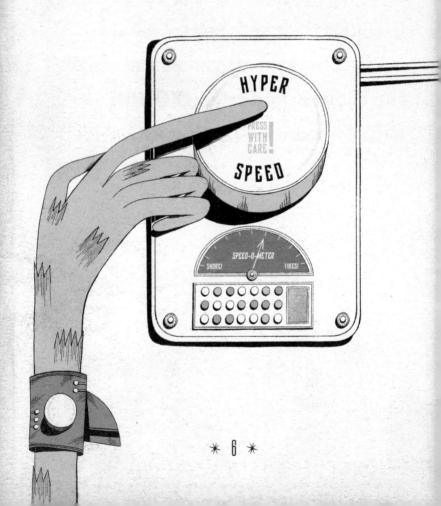

The spaceship shook.

The spaceship wiggled.

The Space Cadets held on tight,
then . . .

3 . . .

2 . . .

1 . . .

WH0OOOOOO

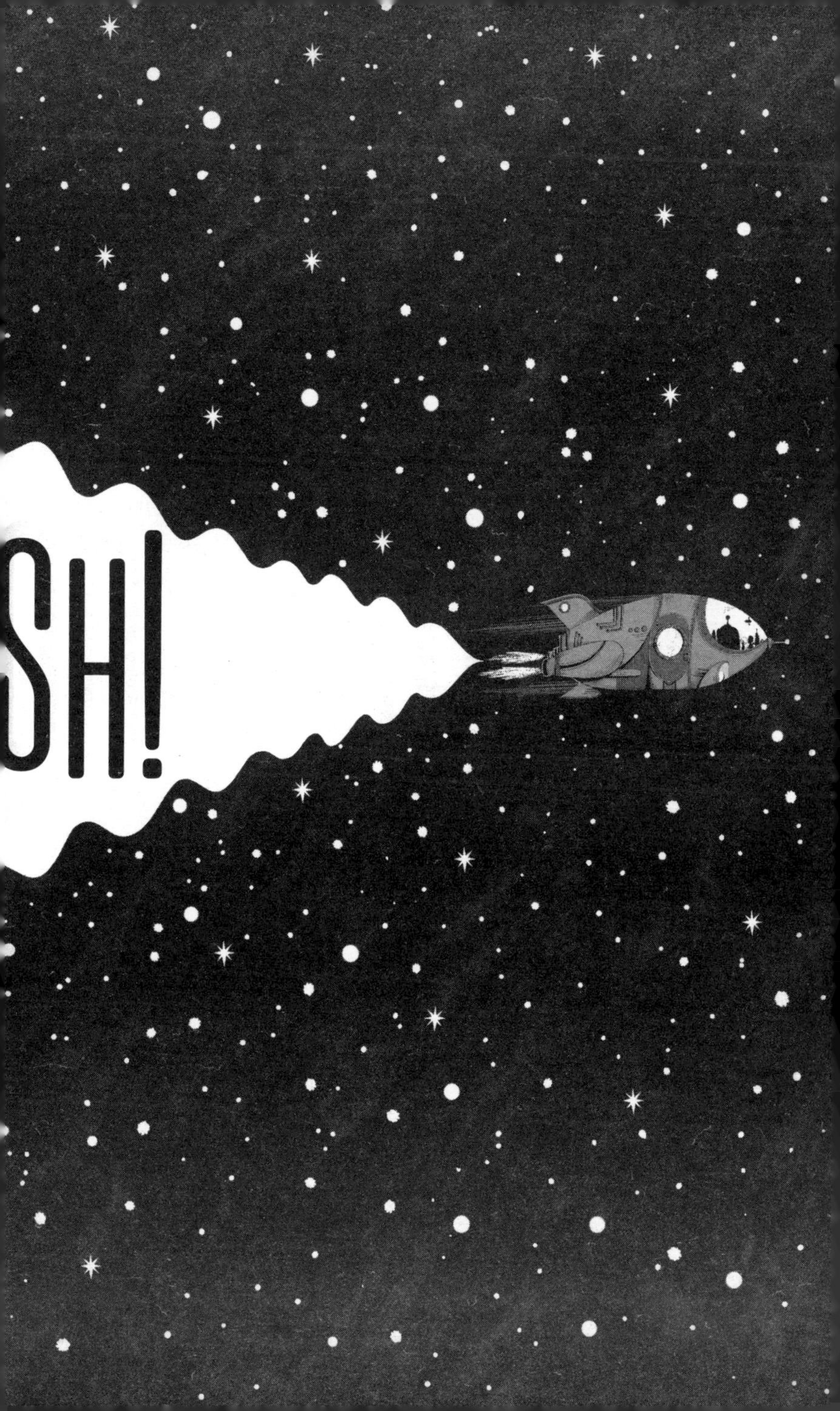
SH!

They blasted off across the galaxy!

Just a few seconds later (because hyper speed is *very speedy*), they had screeched to a halt at the very edge of the Milky Way. The Space Cadets peered out of the spaceship's windows. They all gasped.

'Oh crikey!' said Astrid. She cleaned her specs on her spacesuit and then took another look.

'**Oh dear!**' boomed Beryl.

'Goodness,' quacked Professor Quackers.

'**ZOINK!**' said Zoink (which meant 'Oh bum, this is a disaster!').

And it WAS a disaster.

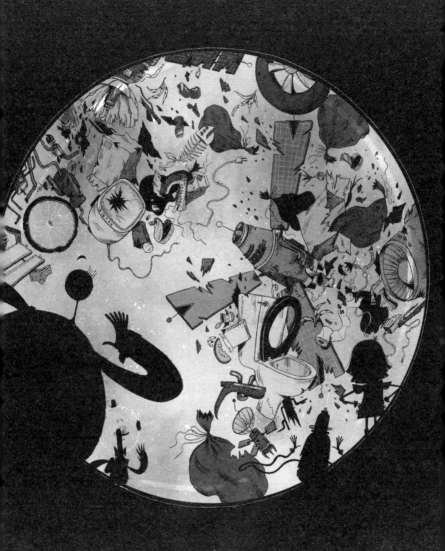

Outside the spaceship, huge piles of space junk floated by. There were heaps of the stuff. Mountains of it! There were bits of old satellites, rusty broken rockets and even a great big ball of sweaty old socks. It was all out there being messy and untidy.

'Maybe this won't be so easy-peasy after all . . .' sighed Astrid.

'This will take aaaaaaages to clean up,' grumbled Beryl.

But Professor Quackers held up a feather. He had two red patches on his cheeks, which meant that he

was excited. 'Worry not,' he said.
'I've got an idea!'

He grabbed his briefcase and
scrabbled around in it. After some
rummaging, he took out a very
strange-looking object indeed.

'This is THE SHRINK BLASTER
10,000!' he announced,
proudly. 'It's my
latest invention.
With a few
blasts of this,
all that space
junk outside
will be made
teeny-tiny.

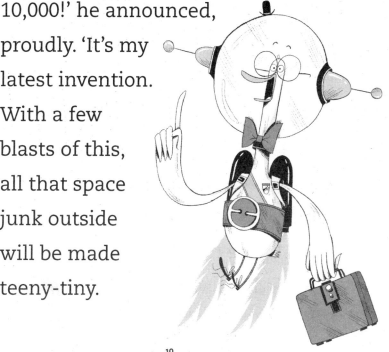

GOSH!

SPARKLE!

GLEAM!

WOW!

Then we can just sweep it up into a bin!'

'We'll have that mess cleared up in minutes!' hooted Astrid. 'Well done, Professor Quackers. You're super clever.' And she gave her friend a high five.

The Space Cadets cheered!

Zoink did a somersault.

Beryl waggled her bottom.

'Let's get our space helmets on, go out there and get blasting,' said Astrid.

Professor Quackers crinkled his beak. 'Well – er . . .' he said nervously. 'We *will* be able to shrink all that rubbish, but only when I've got THE SHRINK BLASTER 10,000 working . . . It's not quite finished yet.'

He scratched his helmet thoughtfully.

'I think maybe I need to re-wangle the splurgle,' he said to himself. 'Or maybe re-jostle the mooter?'

He reached for his toolkit, but just

as he picked up his re-wangler, a red light started to flash in the spaceship.

From the dashboard, an alarm sounded very loudly.

HONK! HONK HONK! HONK HONK!

It made Astrid and the Space Cadets jump.

Beryl covered her ears because she didn't like loud noises.

A voice crackled through the speaker. But it wasn't The Chief.

`Crackle . . . Crackle . . .`

'Hello?' said the mystery voices. 'Is that the Space Cadets?'

Crackle . . . Crackle . . .

'Yes,' said Astrid, politely. 'This is Astrid Atomic speaking.'
'Oh good!' said the voice.

Crackle . . . Crackle . . .

Then it shouted,

'I NEED YOUR HELP!'

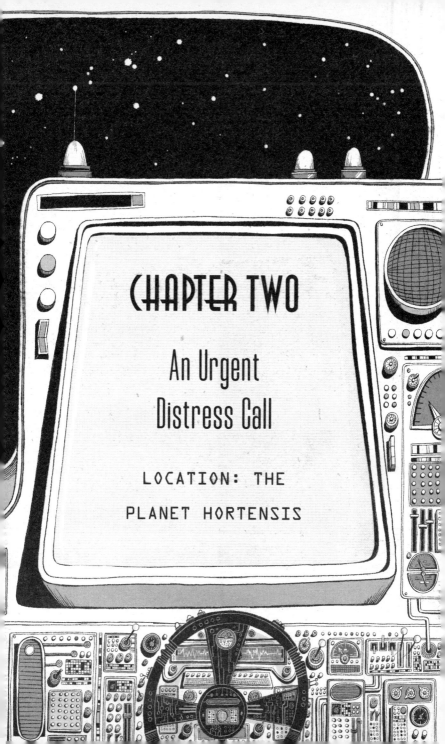

CHAPTER TWO

An Urgent Distress Call

LOCATION: THE
PLANET HORTENSIS

The call was coming from an alien on a planet right over on the other side of the galaxy. Her name was a long list of numbers and shapes and letters, which all translated to mean Flora Mulch. And, oh boy, was Flora Mulch in a panic!

'I've got a BIG problem!' cried Flora Mulch. 'I live on the planet Hortensis, and I need you to come here as fast as you can please! Zoom left at the Three Moons and turn right at the asteroid shaped like a watering can!' And with that, she rang off.

'Oh crikey!' said Astrid. 'I wonder what the problem is. It sounds like an urgent emergency! We'll have to come back to this space junk and solve that problem later. Flora Mulch needs us now.'

The Space Cadets agreed. Flora Mulch sounded like she was in a panic, and Space Cadet Rule Number 1 was:

✳ ALWAYS BE A ✳ HELPER-OUTER.

They didn't lose any time and set off immediately.

CLICK-CLICK! Seat belts on! HOLD ON TIGHT! Red Button pressed!

WHOOOOOOOSH!

'**Oooh!**' said Beryl, as they landed. '**The whole place is like a big, beautiful garden!**'

And she was right.

The Space Cadets hopped out and
looked around. Hortensis was
a round, leafy planet that
smelt of wet earth and
juicy, fruity flowers.

Astrid could see Flora Mulch's house right in the middle of the planet. It looked like a very big ladybird and was surrounded by lovely, lush plants.

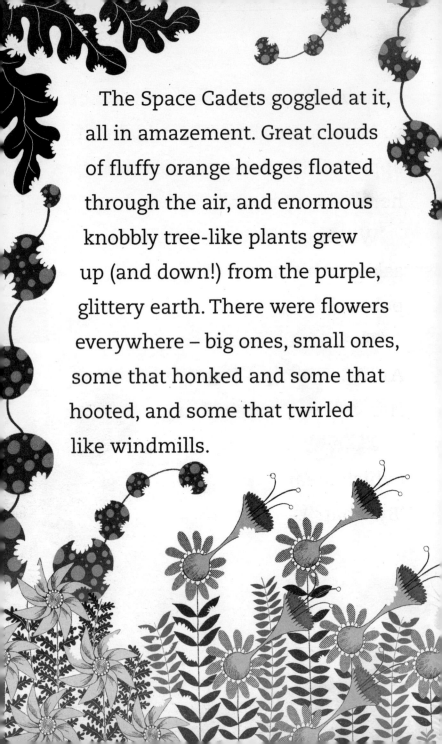

The Space Cadets goggled at it, all in amazement. Great clouds of fluffy orange hedges floated through the air, and enormous knobbly tree-like plants grew up (and down!) from the purple, glittery earth. There were flowers everywhere – big ones, small ones, some that honked and some that hooted, and some that twirled like windmills.

Suddenly, there was the sound of running footsteps and Flora Mulch appeared. 'Thank goodness you're here!' she cried.

'What seems to be the problem?' asked Astrid, striking a heroic poise.

'The plants have been ATTACKED!' said Flora Mulch. Her knees were trembling.

'**ZOINK?**' said Zoink (which meant 'By what?').

'SNAILIENS!' yelped Flora Mulch.

'**Oh I love Snailiens!**' Beryl
squealed. '**They are so cute
and tiny. Can we keep them
as pets?**' She turned to Astrid
and fluttered her eyelashes.

'No, you don't understand!'
said Flora Mulch, all of aquiver.
'These are not ordinary Snailiens.
They are ENORMOUS!'

She pulled back some gigantic,
polka dot leaves and pointed across
the planet. Not far away were five
very large Snailiens. And they
were busily chomping through
everything in sight.

'Today is the Interplanetary Country Fair and my Astro Spuds are in the Oversized Galactic Vegetable Competition,' continued Flora Mulch.

She pointed to the other side of her garden, where, in an overflowing vegetable patch, a pile of large, pink space potatoes were peeking out of the ground.

'I need to load my spuds into my rocket tractor to go to the show. But if I do that, the Snailiens will spot them and come slurping over to gobble them up! I think Astro Spuds are their favourite things to eat.' Flora Mulch's hands shook in her gardening gloves. 'Can you help me?'

Astrid rubbed her nose. 'Hmmm, this IS a conundrum,' she said. Then she put her hands on her hips and nodded in a very determined fashion. 'Don't worry! We'll help you.' Then Astrid turned to Beryl, Zoink and Professor Quackers and called, 'SPACE CADETS ASSEMBLE!'

She paused dramatically.

'It's time for us to make A Plan!'

CHAPTER THREE

Slurpy Like Spaghetti

LOCATION: BEHIND A GUMFUDDLE BUSH ON THE PLANET HORTENSIS

'Let's split up,' said Astrid. 'Zoink and Beryl – you come with me. We'll distract the Snailiens whilst you, Professor Quackers, help Flora Mulch pick her Astro Spuds and get them loaded onto the rocket tractor. Okay?'

The Space Cadets nodded and fist-bumped. Then they hurried off. Astrid, Zoink and Beryl went in one direction, and Professor Quackers and Flora Mulch went in the other.

'**ZOINK?**' said Zoink.

'I'm not sure *how* we'll distract the Snailiens, Zoink . . .' whispered

Astrid, thinking hard. 'Do you have any ideas?'

'**We could cuddle them**,' squeaked Beryl, excitedly. '**And give them kisses?**'

Astrid and Zoink thought this was a good idea at first. But as they got closer to the Snailiens, they realized this was not a good idea at all. The Snailiens were rather large and had huge chomping teeth. They did not look very cuddly at all.

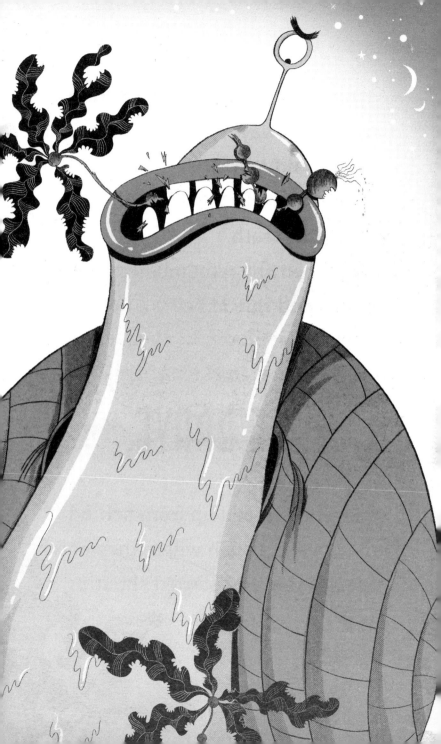

'It's important that we get their attention away from the Astro Spud patch,' said Astrid.

She felt nervous of the huge chomping teeth.

But then she remembered that the second rule of being a Space Cadet was:

 ✷ BE BRAVE. ✷

So she jumped up from behind the hovering bush where they had been hiding and started shouting and waving her arms about.

'Oi, Snailiens! Look over here!'
she cried. 'Not over there! Look
over here instead!'

Zoink and Beryl
leapt up beside
her and started
to copy her.

The Snailiens slowly turned their eyes towards the noise. They looked the Space Cadets up and down and then turned back to what they were doing (which was chomping great chunks out of a blue, blooming Boing-Boing tree).

'Well, that didn't work!' said Astrid, glumly.

'**Why don't we just move them out of the way?**' suggested Beryl.

And before Astrid or Zoink had a chance to respond, Beryl had scampered right over to the creatures and started to heave-ho.

Astrid and Zoink quickly ran
to help her.

The Snailiens were squishy
and they were covered in a sticky,
green goo. Astrid's hands were
soon covered in it. It smelt of very
whiffy old egg sandwiches. Astrid
wrinkled her nose.

'**ZOINK!**' said Zoink (which meant
'Yuck!'). But they got stuck in,
helping their pals with the task of
moving the beasts.

The three Space Cadets pushed
and they pulled, while the Snailiens
carried on chomping and blinking.

They heaved and huffed. After five long, sweaty minutes they had moved the Snailiens . . . nowhere.

'**ZOINK**,' said Zoink, crossly.

Astrid nodded. 'They ARE heavy!' she agreed. She frowned. 'They are too heavy for us to shift. We need another new idea.'

The three Space Cadets had just put their heads together to think, when all of a sudden there came a very loud POP from across the planet.

Astrid, Zoink and Beryl peered around from behind a Snailien's bum to see what had caused the noise. It was Flora Mulch and Professor Quackers – they were pulling the Astro Spuds out of the ground.

The vegetables were tall and pink with a single stalk and a flower on top, and each time one emerged from the earth there was a very loud

POP!

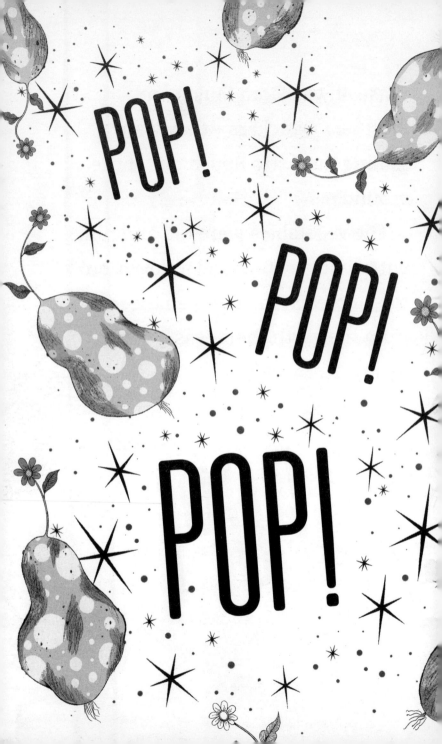

The noise had alerted the Snailiens. All at the same time, they stopped chewing to look.

'Oh crikey!' gasped Astrid.

The Snailiens narrowed their eyes.

'**ZOINK**,' whispered Zoink (which meant 'Uh-oh!').

The Snailiens grinned big, toothy grins.

'**Oh dear! Oh dear!**' cried Beryl, hugging Astrid and Zoink to her very tightly.

The Snailiens started to slither towards the vegetable patch, leaving a sticky, squelchy trail of slime behind them.

They were actually rather speedy.

'Oh crikey!' said Astrid, fascinated. 'They can shift their bottoms very quickly when they want to, can't they?'

She and Beryl were pushed out of the way by two of the creatures. Next to them, another Snailien was so distracted by the sight of the delicious-looking Astro Spuds that it sucked Zoink up by the arm, like they were a piece of spaghetti. Soon, poor Zoink was dangling from its mouth!

Astrid nibbled her lip with worry. Her friend was in danger!

'**ZOINK!**' yelped Zoink (which meant 'Please can somebody help me rather quickly because I appear to be being gobbled up by a large ferocious beast, thank you!').

'Oh crikey!' cried Astrid.

She picked herself up and grabbed Beryl's hand. Together they started to gallop after the Snailiens.

'Quick, Professor Quackers!' she shouted, squelching through the creatures' sticky goo. 'The Snailiens are coming right at you! Do something!'

The Snailiens continued to thunder towards the vegetable patch. One still had Zoink dangling from its mouth. All five sets of beady eyes were glaring greedily at the Astro Spud in Professor Quackers' feathers.

'I . . . I don't know what to do!' he stammered. 'If only these Snailiens weren't so big!'

Then, just as he said that –

PING!

– he had an idea!

'Worry not!' Professor Quackers cried. And he handed the Astro Spud he was holding to Flora Mulch and reached for his briefcase.

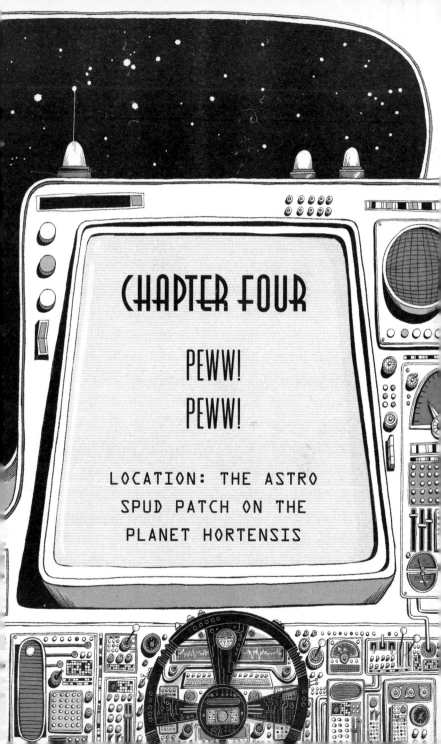

Professor Quackers pulled out THE
SHRINK BLASTER 10,000. 'I'll shrink
the Snailiens!' he shouted.

'But I thought it didn't work yet?'
panted Astrid. She was still hoofing
it after the slippery,
squelchy beasts.

'I'll fix it now!' cried Professor
Quackers.

Quickly, he pulled out his re-wangler
and re-wangled the splurgle.

'There!' he said cheerfully.

He pulled a lever on the side of the
little machine. Like magic, the whole
thing lit up and started to hum.

He aimed it carefully at the
Snailiens.

'Duck!' he said to his pals.

'**We know you're a duck**,'
said Beryl.

'I mean TAKE COVER!' said
Professor Quackers.

Astrid and Beryl didn't need

telling twice. They tumbled into the roughty-tufty undergrowth. Flora Mulch buried her head in a hole in the ground. Still dangling from a Snailien's mouth, Zoink put their free hand over their helmet and closed their eyes.

'Ready! Aim! FIRE!' hollered Professor Quackers.

He thumped the big button on top of THE SHRINK BLASTER 10,000.

PEWW! PEWW!

went the laser. There was a bright flash.

There was a loud

BANG!

The air filled with clouds of stinky smoke that smelt of burnt turnips.

Zoink landed beside Astrid with a flump. Their arm was sopping wet with soggy Snailien dribble.

'Has it worked?' asked Professor Quackers through the fog. He'd been sent flying by the explosion and was now upside down in a bush.

'Um . . . I'm not sure,' said Astrid.

She hopped up and wafted her hands about to try to clear the thick, smelly haze.

'It must have done,' she said, eventually. 'There are no signs of them anywhere. You must have shrunk them down so small that

we can't see them at all. Well done,
Professor Quackers!'

Astrid was just about to find
her fellow Space Cadets for a
celebratory wiggly-bottom dance
when the ground beneath her moon
boots started to tremble.

It shook.

Then it shook again.

Somewhere nearby there was a terrifically loud grumbling noise.

Zoink appeared by Astrid's side. '**ZOINK!**' they said.

'I don't know *what's* happening . . .' replied Astrid, biting her lip. She was starting to worry a bit. 'But I don't think it can be very good.'

And it wasn't.

The smelly, turnip smoke started to clear. Astrid could just make out some very large shapes.

The shapes got clearer.

Astrid's mouth dropped open.

'Oh crikey!' she said, suddenly realizing what had happened. 'Um . . . Professor Quackers?' she called. 'You didn't shrink the Snailiens. You've made them . . .

GINORMOUS!'

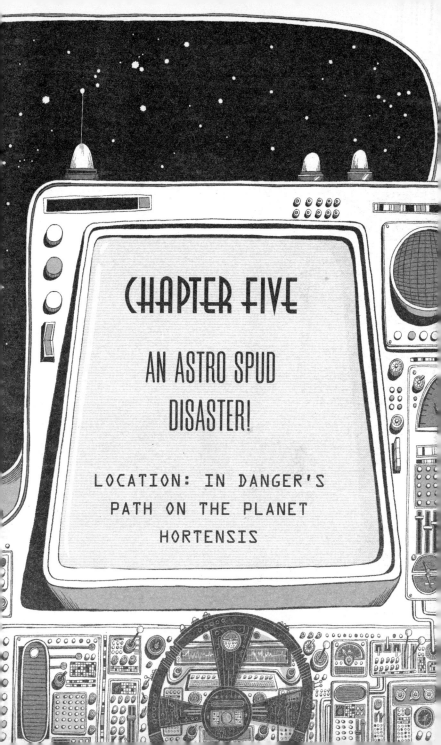

The Snailiens were now HUGE!

HUGER than HUGE, in fact!

They were ENORMOUS!

They were GIGANTIC!

They were GARGANTUAN!

They were VERY LARGE INDEED!

They swept along the ground, making it tremble and shake like jelly. Their big squishy bodies crushed everything in their path, chomping all the plants and trees in their way.

'**Aww**,' squeaked Beryl, enchanted by them.

They towered over the Boing-Boing trees, pulled them completely out of the earth and gobbled them up like they weren't trees at all but just teeny-tiny carrot sticks.

'**Oh!**' said Beryl. '**Look how cute they are!**'

'They aren't cute!' cried Flora Mulch. 'They are destroying my whole planet! And look – they are heading right for my prize-winning Astro Spuds! Quick, Space Cadets! Do something, before they eat everything up!'

Professor Quackers came floating into view, having escaped from the

bush
where
THE SHRINK
BLASTER
10,000's blast
had thrown him.

'Can you do anything,
Professor Quackers?'
asked Astrid. She knew
her friend was super
clever – if anyone could
fix this, he could.

'Worry not!' Professor Quackers
quacked. 'I can fix this!'

He ferreted about in his briefcase
and whipped out his re-jostler.

Quickly, he fiddled about with some very complicated-looking bits of machinery on his special invention.

'Quick!' yelped Astrid. She'd spotted that the Snailiens were hurrying towards the Astro Spuds again.

'Ready!' said Professor Quackers. Once more, he aimed THE SHRINK BLASTER 10,000 at the creatures and thumped the big button.

Lasers fired!

PEWW! PEWW!

A FLASH!

A BANG!

A RUMBLE!

Another cloud of
stinky turnip smoke
slowly cleared.

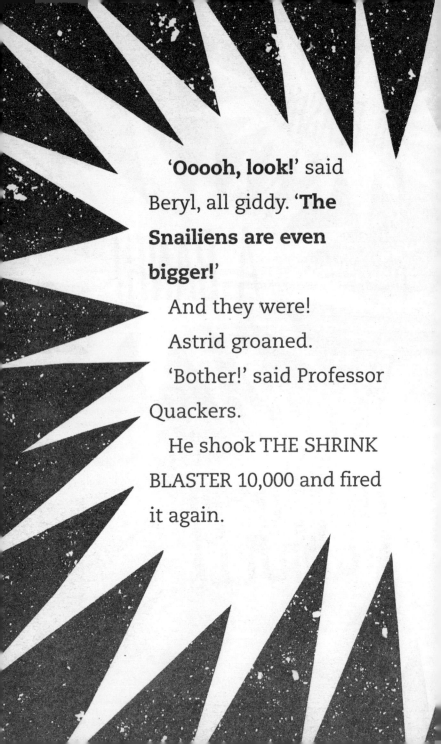

'**Ooooh, look!**' said Beryl, all giddy. '**The Snailiens are even bigger!**'

And they were!

Astrid groaned.

'Bother!' said Professor Quackers.

He shook THE SHRINK BLASTER 10,000 and fired it again.

AT!

A third cloud of stinky turnip
smoke slowly cleared.

'Oh crikey!' yelped Astrid, wiping
green liquid from her helmet. 'I think
you need to stop firing THE SHRINK
BLASTER 10,000, Professor Quackers!
It's only making them bigger!'

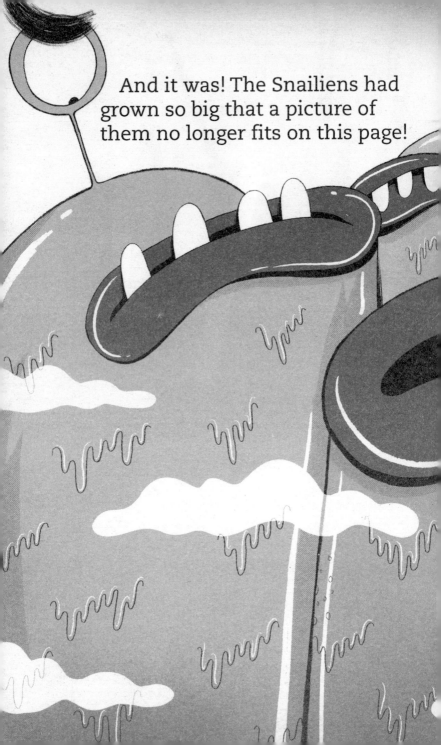

And it was! The Snailiens had grown so big that a picture of them no longer fits on this page!

Sticky Snailien goo was all over the place, and Astrid and the Space Cadets were completely covered in the stuff.

'Worry not!' said Professor Quackers, sounding quite worried.

He fumbled with his briefcase.

'I . . . er . . . I know I can fix this. I'll be able to shrink them. Maybe I need to re-wangle the mooter this time?' he muttered to himself.

But before he could re-wangle anything, the Boing-Boing tree beside him tumbled to the ground.

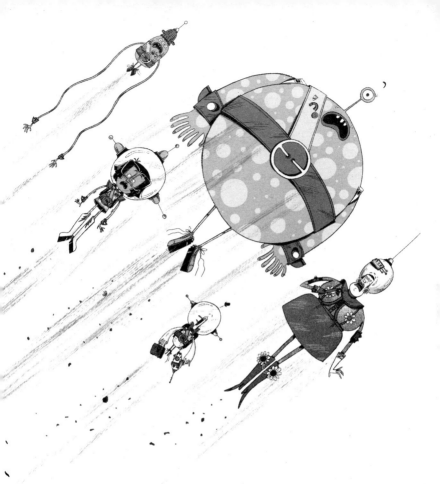

It THUMPED down hard to the forest
floor, sending Flora Mulch and the
Space Cadets flying through the air
like they'd been catapulted!

They all landed in a thick patch of Twirl Petal flowers. THE SHRINK BLASTER 10,000 crashed beside them and – SMASH! – broke into lots and lots of pieces. They wouldn't be able to use it again, that was for sure!

Across the planet, Astrid could see that the Snailiens had broken into the Astro Spud patch. They were looking very pleased with themselves.

'Oh no! Oh no! Oh no!' said Flora Mulch, very sadly. 'Look! Those creatures are in my vegetable patch now! My prize-winning Astro Spuds will be gobbled up. Everything is ruined! This is a disaster!'

Astrid frowned, thinking hard. It certainly all seemed like a disaster, but she had to do something! Flora Mulch had worked super hard to grow such big, beautiful Astro Spuds. All that work couldn't go to waste.

Space Cadets solved *ALL* problems – big or small. The Snailiens were certainly a VERY BIG problem indeed, but she was sure there was also a solution.

'Come on, Space Cadets!' she said, urgently. 'We can do this! We just need to think!'

'**I can't think of anything,**' said Beryl woozily. '**I'm too dizzy from flying through the air!**'

She stood up, and Astrid couldn't help but giggle. Beryl looked very funny. The sticky Snailien goo had stuck lots of loose petals to her poor head.

'Tee-hee!' Astrid laughed. 'Oh Beryl, you look just like—'

She had been going to say that Beryl looked like a big beautiful Astro Spud. But she stopped before she could finish her sentence.

An idea had suddenly pinged into her head.

Astrid's plan was underway.

At the controls of the spaceship, she reached for the steering wheel. 'Is everyone ready?' she cried out of the window.

Below the spaceship, near the vegetable patch, Professor Quackers and Flora Mulch poked their heads out from the bush they were hiding in.

'Yes!' said Professor Quackers.

'Yes!' said Flora Mulch.

'**ZOINK!**' cried Zoink (which meant 'Yes!').

'**Um . . . I think so!**' called Beryl.

'Good,' said Astrid. 'Then let's go'

We'll distract the Snailiens, and you –
Professor Quackers and Flora Mulch
– you save the Astro Spuds, OK?'

'I hope this works,' squeaked
Flora Mulch.

So do I, thought Astrid. But she
didn't say it out loud.

Instead she CLICK-
CLICKED her seat belt
and looked very
determined.
Then she
pressed
some
buttons
on the

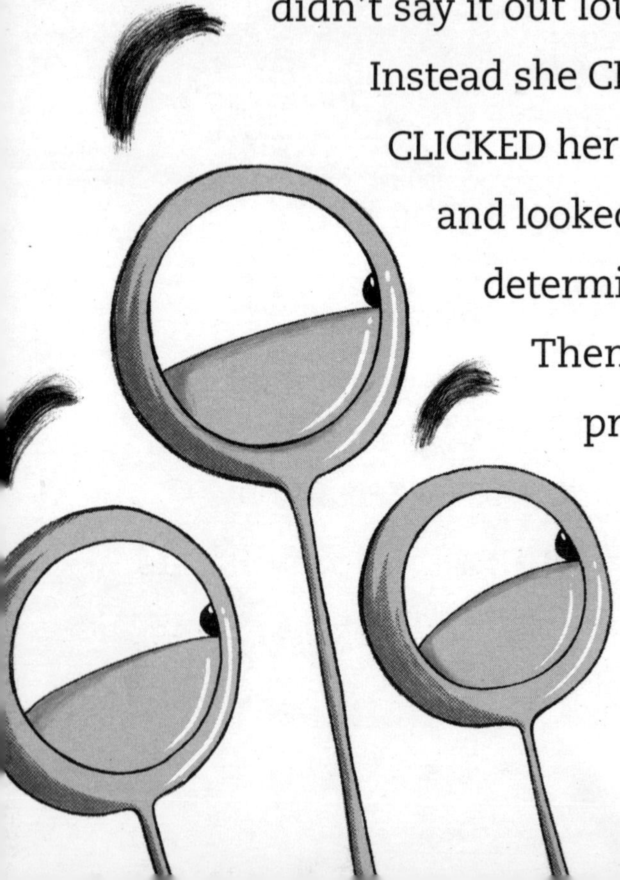

spaceship's
dashboard,
pulled a
lever and
tilted the
steering wheel
towards her. The
rockets fired at
the back of the
vehicle and slowly the entire
spaceship rose majestically up
into the air.

Underneath the spaceship,
dangling from the underside by
their feet, was Zoink. In their hands
dangled Beryl. With the flower petals

around her head, she really did look JUST like a lovely Astro Spud.

Astrid pulled the spaceship higher into the sky. It flew over the Snailiens' heads and waggled Zoink and Beryl in front of the creature's eyes. Her whole plan revolved around the Snailiens being tricked into thinking Beryl was something delicious to eat.

But the Snailiens hadn't noticed Beryl. They were too busy licking their chops and giggling with excitement.

'It's not working!' cried Flora Mulch from the ground in a panic.

'Quick, Beryl!' said Astrid. 'Do

something enticing and potatoey.'

Beryl thought fast, then she let out a very loud whistle. '**Cooee! Snailiens!**' she shouted. '**Look at me, I'm a delicious Astro Spud! Yum yum!**'

Well, that worked a treat! All five of the Snailiens' heads turned together to look at the spaceship.

Their eyes lit up.

They licked their lips.

One of them tried to nibble at the dangling potato, but it was *just* out of their reach.

But that didn't stop them!

There was a loud TRUMPING

noise and flames flared from somewhere near the region of the Snailiens' bums. Suddenly, the gigantic beasts lifted slowly into the air.

'They're following us!' cried Astrid from the spaceship, ever so excited. 'It's working! My plan is working!'

'**Don't let them bite my bottom!**' yelped Beryl nervously. The Snailiens were getting a little bit too close to her bum for her liking.

But, of course, Astrid wouldn't allow that. As soon as the Snailiens got near to her friend, she pulled the spaceship up higher, making sure that Beryl was always out of their reach.

Slowly but surely, Astrid led the hungry Snailiens away from the planet Hortensis.

'Quick, Professor Quackers!' cried Astrid, as soon as all five Snailiens were up in the air. 'Rescue those Astro Spuds!'

TRRRUUUUUU

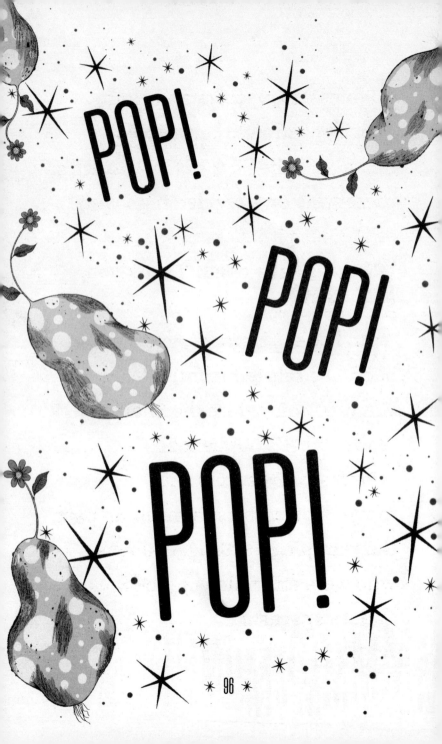

POP!

POP!

POP!

96

Professor Quackers and Flora Mulch got straight to work.

In a jiffy, the back of Flora Mulch's rocket tractor was piled high with enormous pink potatoes.

'Hurrah!' she cried. 'Thank you, Space Cadets!'

'All in a day's work!' Astrid called back. She saluted jauntily. 'Now, you hurry off before the Snailiens realize what's happened!'

Professor Quackers used his moon boots to blast himself up past the trumping, floating Snailiens who were still following the Space Cadet's spaceship.

He helped Zoink and Beryl safely inside and together the Space Cadets watched as Flora Mulch's rocket tractor zoomed off across the galaxy.

'Great work, team,' said Astrid with a big grin.

They all had a very quick wiggly-bottom dance in celebration.

'Now,' she said. 'Let's get out of here!'

They scrambled back into their seats and CLICK-CLICKED their seat belts in place.

Zoink took over the controls and pressed the big, red HYPER SPEED button.

The spaceship shook.

The spaceship trembled.

3...

2...

1...

Off it sped, right away from the
planet Hortensis.

WHOOOOOOOO

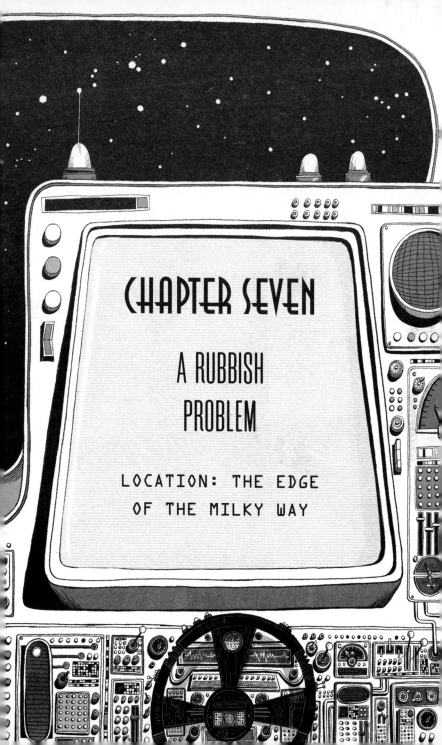

'Oh crikey!'
said Astrid as the space-
ship screeched to a halt.
'With all that excitement over
the Astro Spuds and the Snailiens,
I'd forgotten about this mess!'

She pointed out of the window
at the piles of rubbish floating
about at the edge of the Milky
Way. There seemed to be even
more rubbish now than there
had been earlier.

'And THE SHRINK BLASTER 10,000
is completely broken. We can't even
use that to help,' said Professor
Quackers glumly.

Zoink put their hands on their hips. '**ZOINK**,' they said.

Astrid nodded. 'Yes, Zoink, you're right. We'll just have to put on some rubber gloves and get cracking.'

She began hunting about in cupboards for the Space Cadets' cleaning supply box.

'I just hope we can get at least SOME of it tidied before The Chief calls,' she called over her shoulder. But no sooner had she said it than The Chief's face fizzled into view on the screen.

CRACKLE . . . CRACKLE . . .

'**Greetings, Space Cadets!**'
she said. '**How are you getting on? Is the Milky Way tidy again?**'

CRACKLE . . . CRACKLE . . .

'**Oh dear!**' continued The Chief. Her eyes had slid to the windows of the spaceship, where she could clearly see the heaps of garbage outside.

Astrid sighed sadly and said, 'I'm afraid we haven't managed to get any of that mess tidied up.' She felt very disappointed.

'**We got distracted by another little problem**,' said Beryl.

'Well, a BIG problem really,' added Professor Quackers.

The Space Cadets quickly filled The Chief in with everything that had happened on the planet Hortensis.

The Chief listened to their story.

'**Goodness me!**' said The Chief at the end. '**You've been busy! Don't worry about—**'

She was suddenly interrupted by a loud noise.

CHOMP!
CHOMP!

'Pardon?' said Astrid to The Chief. 'We can't hear you.'

'I said you've been busy! Don't—' fizzled The Chief. But once again she was cut off by a strange sound.

CHOMP!
CHOMP!

'**Space Cadets?**' cried The Chief, over the disruption. '**What is that dreadful noise? It sounds like someone eating!**'

And indeed it did. But where was it coming from?

The Space Cadets peered out of the spaceship's windows.

'**Look!**' squealed Beryl, giddily.

The Space Cadets followed her pointing finger.

Astrid grinned when she saw what was outside.

'It's the Snailiens!' cried Professor Quackers.

'**ZOINK!**' said Zoink.

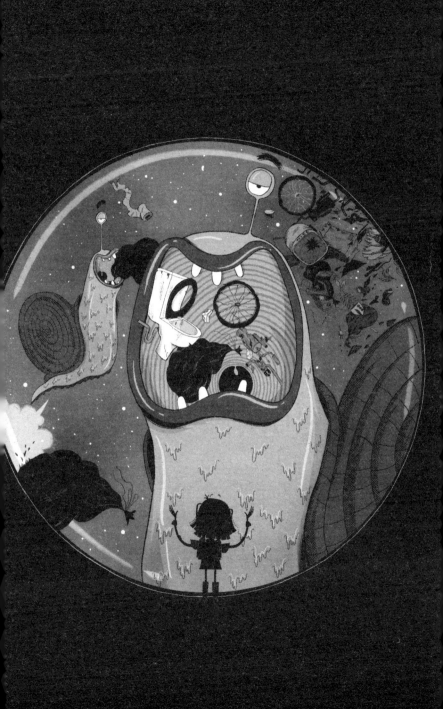

'That's right, Zoink!' said Astrid. 'They must have followed us here and – look! – they are chomping away at all the space junk!'

She swizzled the screen around so that The Chief could see what was happening too.

Floating about in the darkness, all five of the enormous Snailiens were very busy. They were gobbling happily away at all the rubbish!

'Crikey!' said Astrid, with a grin. She threw her arms around her best friends as they watched the Snailiens through the window.

'They'll have all of that eaten up in no time! I think the Snailiens like space junk even more than they like Astro Spuds.'

'**Fantastic!**' hooted The Chief. '**I was just about to say don't worry about that garbage — you could tidy that up another day — but it seems you've found a brilliant solution to the problem! Well done, Space Cadets. It gives me great pleasure to award you a gold star each for your star chart!**'

The Space Cadets cheered and did another wiggly-bottom dance in celebration.

'**Oh! What's this?**' said The Chief suddenly. From wherever she was, there came the zip-zip sound of something printing.

The Chief held up a sheet of paper.

'**It's a message from Flora Mulch,**' she said. '**It reads: Dear The Chief. Please tell the Space Cadets that my Astro Spuds won first prize at the Interplanetary Country Fair and thank them for all their** help today. I couldn't have rescued my veg without them!'

The Space Cadets cheered again.

'I think that calls for another gold star each! Excellent work, Space Cadets! I'm very proud of you!'

The Chief waved and disappeared from the screen.

There was a flash and a fizzle in the spaceship and two gold stars EACH appeared and stuck themselves to the Space Cadets' star chart.

'**Oooh!**' squeaked Beryl, excitedly. '**We're two stars closer to the Great Galaxy Prize!**'

The Space Cadets pals took a moment to think dreamily about doughnuts. Then they danced around the cabin wiggling their bottoms.

Suddenly, they were interrupted by a beeping noise. It sounded a bit like an alarm clock going off.

'Oh crikey!' said Astrid. 'It's time for me to go. Until tomorrow night, team!'

She gave her friends a great big, squeeeeeeeezy hug and a fist bump each.

Then she hopped into the transporter pod and with a KABOOM! she went home.

Back in her bedroom, Astrid crept out of her wardrobe and wiped the last bit of Snailien goo off her hands. She put her pyjamas back on over her uniform. Then she got into bed.

'Great work, Space Cadets!' she said sleepily to herself as she closed her eyes.

Then she yawned and fell asleep, wondering what adventure tomorrow night would bring.

THE END
(of THIS mission . . .)

CRACKLE . . .

CRACKLE . . .

TURN THE PAGE TO READ THE FIRST
CHAPTER OF ASTRID'S NEXT ADVENTURE...

ASTRID AND THE SPACE CADETS!

Race from Planet Peril

COMING JULY 2024!

A MESSAGE FROM THE SPACE CADETS' BOSS, THE CHIEF:

CRACKLE . . . CRACKLE . . .

'Greetings, Space Cadets! And welcome to another starlit day here in the universe!

'The mission I have for you is a dangerous one. You'll have to be brave.

'Today is the day of the Supersonic Saturn Spin Race. Lots of spaceships and rockets will be racing around Saturn's ring. The winner of the race gets the priceless Supersonic Saucer.

'Your mission is to go to Planet Peril, fetch the Supersonic Saucer from the safe it's kept in and deliver it to Commander Xander Zoom on Saturn, ready for him to present it to the winner of the race.

'I'm sending you the top-secret passcode you'll need to open up the vault where the Supersonic Saucer is kept.

'And remember, if you complete your task, you'll get another gold star for your cosmic star chart. The more stars on your star chart, the closer you are to getting the Great Galaxy Prize!

'Good luck, Space Cadets! I know you can do it!'

CRACKLE . . . CRACKLE . . .

'Collect the saucer for the Supersonic Saturn Spin Race and get it to Commander Xander Zoom at the finishing line, ready to be handed to the winner,' said Astrid, going over their mission. 'That sounds easy-peasy – we'll get that done in a jiffy!'

But Professor Quackers wasn't convinced. He crinkled his beak, all worried. His bow tie spun round in circles, which meant he was very nervous.

'I'm not sure it will be,' he fussed. 'The Chief said this mission could be dangerous!'

Astrid thought for a second. 'Yes,' she said slowly. 'The Chief did say that . . .'

'**Maybe we should take a look at what Planet Peril is like before we get there?**' suggested Beryl. '**So we are prepared.**'

'Good idea!' exclaimed Astrid.

Zoink quickly did some tip-tapping on a keyboard and up came a picture of Planet Peril on the computer screen. It was a small, red planet, not too far away.

'**ZOINK**,' said Zoink.

'You're right, Zoink,' agreed Astrid. 'It doesn't look very dangerous at all!'

But just then a warning sign flashed on the screen. Arrows appeared, pointing out several very important bits of information. To get to the vault where the Supersonic Saucer was kept, the Space Cadets would have to . . .

1. FLY UNDER BOILING-HOT LAVA WATERFALLS.

2. ZOOM THROUGH FIELDS OF FLAMING FLOWERS THAT SPIT GREAT BALLS OF FIRE.

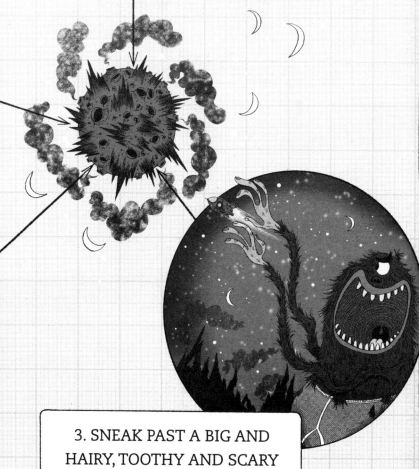

PLANET PERIL!
DANGER! BEWARE! AVOID! BE VERY CAREFUL!

VOTED THE WORST PLACE TO PICNIC IN THE ENTIRE UNIVERSE!

3. SNEAK PAST A BIG AND HAIRY, TOOTHY AND SCARY MONSTER WHO GUARDS THE CAVE WHERE THE VAULT IS LOCATED.

'Oh crikey!' said Astrid. 'That *does* sound dangerous.' She looked around at the other Space Cadets. 'We'll just have to do what The Chief said and be brave. Remember – we're the Space Cadets and no problem is too big for us!'

The rest of the Space Cadets cheered. Then they set about making sure they had everything they needed for the perilous journey ahead.

'For the lava waterfalls,' said Professor Quackers, 'we'll need to use these new Lava-Repellent Umbrellas I invented last week.'

He pressed a big orange button and – WHIZZ-CLICK! – out of the roof of the spaceship shot seven silver umbrellas that opened up with a flap.

'They're brilliant!' declared Astrid, giving her friend two thumbs up.

'CHECK,' said Professor Quackers, pretending to tick them off a list.

'And to deal with those fireball-spitting flowers,' said Astrid, 'we'll need our Wallopers!'

She pulled a lever on the dashboard and – CLICK-WHIZZ! – from the sides of the spaceship came several robotic arms, each holding a tennis racket that swished and flicked.

'CHECK!' said Astrid.

'**ZOINK!**' Zoink added (which meant 'And luckily for us I filled up the tank just yesterday so that we have lots of rocket fuel to dash past that monster and get back right across the galaxy to Saturn!'). Then they said, '**ZOINK!**' (which meant 'CHECK!').

'So we're all ready for our mission!' said Astrid, with a grin.

'**Almost ready** . . .' replied Beryl.

'Oh!' said Professor Quackers, with a frown. 'What are we missing?'

'**Meteor milkshakes and moon muffins!**' said Beryl, with a lovely big grin.

'Oh crikey!' exclaimed Astrid. 'What do we need those for, Beryl?'

'**For our packed lunch of course!**' Beryl squeaked excitedly. And right on cue her tummy rumbled. '**Being brave is hungry work!**'

Astrid laughed. Now that Beryl had mentioned it, she could do with a snack. Astrid loved how clever Beryl was at thinking of good plans. That's why they were best pals.

'Okay,' said Astrid. 'Let's make a quick detour to the Big Bang Diner

before we dash to Planet Peril.
We've got a little bit of time before
the Supersonic Saturn Spin Race
begins.'

And so the Space Cadets got
ready. They CLICK-CLICKED their
seat belts. Zoink was the driver, so
they took the controls and pressed
a big red button on the dashboard
labelled 'HYPER SPEED'.

The spaceship shook.

The spaceship wiggled.

The Space Cadets held on tight, then . . .

3 . . .

2 . . .

1 . . .

ACKNOWLEDGEMENTS

Making a book is a very complex thing and not something you can do all by yourself. It takes a lot of hard work by a great number of people, and I am very grateful to have the best team helping me make mine. As such the following Space Cadets are awarded a gold star for their Intergalactic Star Charts:

⭐ For Excellent Editing and ⭐
Story Management:
Cate Augustin

⭐ For Out-of-This-World ⭐
Design and Visual Magic:
Becky Chilcott

⭐ For Perfect Publicity: ⭐
Clare Hall-Craggs

⭐ For Marvellous Marketing: ⭐
Cheyney Smith

⭐ For Bookmaking ⭐
Production Wizardry:
Farzana Adlington

⭐ For Astounding ⭐
Audiobook Administration:
Nick Griffiths

⭐ For her Show-Stopping ⭐
Audiobook Performance:
Claire Morgan

⭐ A Gold Star is also ⭐
awarded to the following:

The Macmillan Children's Books
Sales and Rights departments
Alyx Price
Michelle Young
Gaby Morgan
Amy Boxshall

Caroline Thomson

Emma O'Donovan

 And finally a PLATINUM  star is awarded to Agent Extraordinaire and Chief: Tamlyn Francis

ABOUT THE AUTHOR-ILLUSTRATOR

Alex T. Smith is the creator of the bestselling Claude fiction series for early readers, as well as the much-loved *How Winston Delivered Christmas*, for which an animated film is currently in development. His other Christmas books include the sequel *How Winston Came Home for Christmas*, *The Grumpus* and the witty retellings of *The Nutcracker* and *The Twelve Days of Christmas*, which are set to become future Christmas classics.

Alex lives in the UK, under the watchful eye of his small canine companions and a flock of unruly chickens.

ALSO AVAILABLE:

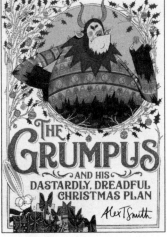

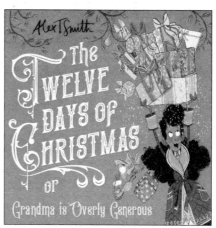